READING IS FUN

FOR: msjoh

FROM: David

USBORNE BOOKS & MORE

THIS CANDLEWICK BOOK BELONGS TO:

_____

_____

_____

For Mum and Dad

The author and publisher would like
to thank Sue Ellis at the Centre for Literacy in
Primary Education, Martin Jenkins, and Paul Harrison
for their invaluable input and guidance
during the making of this book.

First U.S. paperback edition 2009

Library of Congress Cataloging-in-Publication Data is available.
Library of Congress Catalog Card Number 2007052195
ISBN 978-0-7636-4025-5 (hardcover)
ISBN 978-0-7636-4513-7 (paperback)

10 9 8 7 6 5 4 3 2 1

Printed in China

This book was typeset in ITCKabel.
The illustrations were created digitally.

Candlewick Press
99 Dover Street
Somerville, Massachusetts 02144

visit us at www.candlewick.com

CANDLEWICK PRESS

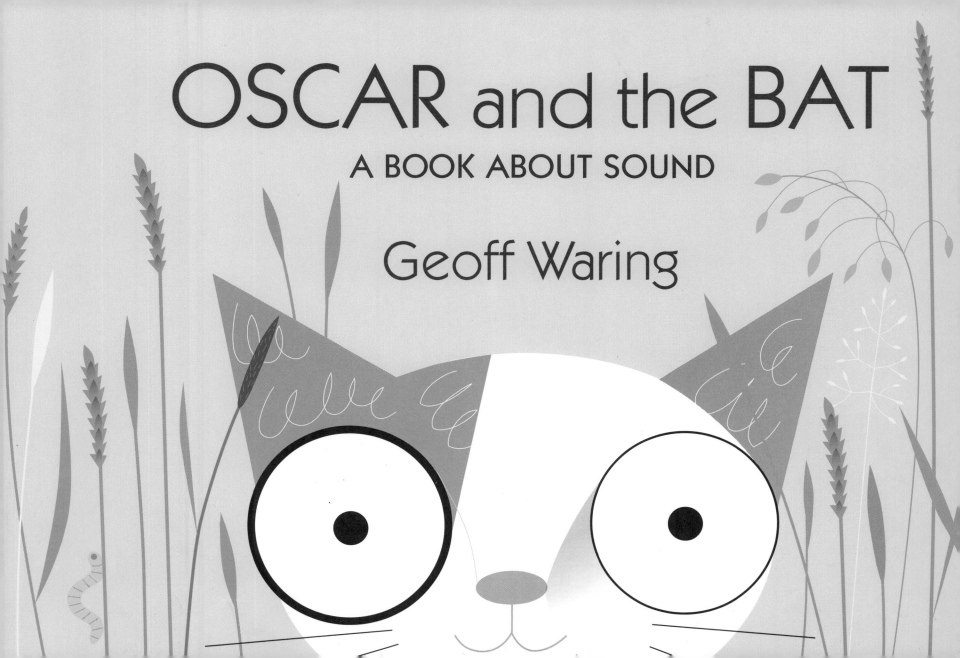

OSCAR and the BAT
A BOOK ABOUT SOUND

Geoff Waring

One summer evening in the meadow,
Oscar heard a new sound. He looked around
to see who was making it.

Bat swooped by.
"It's the baby blackbirds," he said. "Their nest
is over there in the bush."
"Oh," said Oscar. "I can hear them, even though
I can't see them!"
"Yes," said Bat. "Our ears help us know
what's around us, even when our eyes can't."

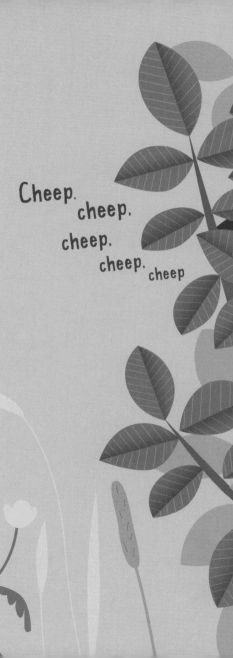

Cheep.
cheep.
cheep.
cheep.
cheep

♫ Sreeeeee—sree—tweee ♫

Then Oscar heard another sound.
This time he could see who was making it.

"The blackbird's singing to warn other blackbirds
to stay away from his nest," Bat said.

Oscar thought it was the most beautiful sound
he had ever heard.

"I wish I could sing like a blackbird!" he said.

"Kittens can make other sounds," Bat said. "So can bats!"

Squeak

Meow

"We make sounds in our throats," Bat went on, "but some animals talk with different parts of their bodies."

Many male grasshoppers talk to female grasshoppers by rubbing their wings together.

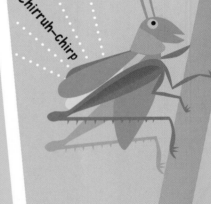

Chirruh-chirp

Some cockroaches hiss to one another through holes along their sides.

Hiss, hiss

Hiss, hiss

When they nest, some male hummingbirds make a loud sound with their wings to warn other birds away.

Whistle

Whirrrr

Rattle, rattle

Click whistle Squeak

Bottlenose dolphins send messages to one another underwater through their blowholes.

The tips of rattlesnakes' tails have hard connecting ridges. If other animals come too close, the snakes lift and shake their tails.

11

"Are all sounds 'talking sounds'?" Oscar asked. "Lots are," Bat said, "but almost everything makes a sound when it moves. Close your eyes and listen. What can you hear moving in the meadow?"

Grass makes no sound when it's still, but it swishes when the wind moves it.

Swish

Swish

Swish

Swish

Swish

Swish

Brroooom

Machines are still and silent
until they are switched on.
Then their engines move
and make noises.

Still water in a pond is silent,
but moving water makes sounds.

Gurgle,
gurgle

Gurgle,   gurgle

Gurgle,
gurgle

Rumble. rumble Rumble. rumble

Oscar could hear another sound. It was in the sky.
"What's that rumbling?" he asked.

"Thunder," said Bat. "There's a storm coming.
Even though it's far away, we can still hear
the thunder because it's such a big sound."

Rumble, rumble   **Rumble, rumble**   **Rumble, rumble**

Oscar opened his eyes. "It's getting louder!" he said.

"The thunder's coming this way," Bat said.
"The closer it is to us, the louder it sounds to us."

Rumble, CRA

"And when a big noise is very near . . .

SH!

it sounds very loud indeed!"
Bat shouted as Oscar leaped away.

Safe under the leaves, Oscar
listened to raindrops falling.
"The rain is very near
too," he said, "but it
isn't scary."

Pitter, patter

Pitter, patter

Pitter, patter

"The rain is making a
gentle sound," Bat said,
"not a harsh sound
like the thunder."

19

When the rain stopped, Oscar put out his head to listen. "Is the thunder going away now?" he asked.

"Yes," said Bat. "The farther it is from us, the quieter it sounds to us."

Then it was gone.

"I can't hear anything," Oscar whispered.

"No," whispered Bat. "This is silence—
or it would be if we weren't whispering!"

But just then . . .

"The cow sounds a bit like the thunder!" said Oscar.

"Yes," said Bat. "Cows make a deep sound.
It's low and rumbly. It isn't high and squeaky,
like the sound the baby birds made."

Trippa-treep-trippa-trrrr

24

Now the blackbird started to sing again.

"That's still my favorite sound," said Oscar.
"It keeps changing. And it's never too loud
and scary or too high and squeaky.
It's just right, like music!"

And he started to purr.

Purrrrrrrrrr

"And that's *my* favorite sound," said Oscar's mother, who had come to fetch him.

But Oscar and Bat were listening so hard, they didn't notice.

Thinking about sound

In the meadow, Oscar found out about these things:

Listening

Our ears help us to know what's
happening around us.

Cheep,
cheep

Cheep,
cheep,
cheep

We can hear
things we can't see.

We can tell how far away
something is . . . Rumble, rumble

or how near
it is. Rumble, rumble

What can you hear around you now?

Is it easier to listen if you close your eyes?

Making sounds

All sorts of things make sounds—
living things and other things.

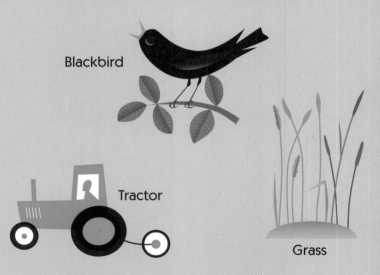

Blackbird

Tractor

Grass

Place your fingers on your throat
and sing or say something.
How does the sound feel?

Different sounds

There are many kinds of sounds.

Some opposites help us to think about their differences.

Rumble, rumble
Harsh

Pitter, patter
Gentle

Mooooooo!
Deep

Cheep, cheep,
High

CRASH!
Scary

♪ Chirrrr-churra-chirrup ♪
Beautiful

What are your favorite sounds?

Index

Look up the pages
to find out about
these "sound" things.

big 14, 16

deep 23, 29

ears 7, 28

gentle 19, 29

harsh 19, 29

hearing 7, 9, 12, 14, 28

high 23, 25, 29

listening 12, 18, 20, 27, 28

loud 11, 15–17, 25

moving 12–13

silent 13, 21

talking 10–12, 21, 28

Oscar thinks sound is great! Do you think so, too?

Geoff Waring studied graphics in college and worked as an art director at *Elle*, *Red*, and *Vogue Australia* and as design director of *British Vogue*. He is currently creative director of *Glamour* magazine. He is the author and illustrator of the Oscar books, as well as the illustrator of *Black Meets White* by Justine Fontes. He says that the Oscar books are based on his own cat, Oskar. Geoff Waring lives in London.